John Brownlie

Zionward

hymns of the pilgrim life

John Brownlie

Zionward
hymns of the pilgrim life

ISBN/EAN: 9783337294922

Printed in Europe, USA, Canada, Australia, Japan

Cover: Foto ©Andreas Hilbeck / pixelio.de

More available books at **www.hansebooks.com**

ZIONWARD

HYMNS OF THE PILGRIM LIl

BY THE

REV. JOHN BROWNLIE,

MINISTER OF THE FREE CHURCH, PORTPATRICK.

LONDON:

JAMES NISBET & CO., 21 BERNERS STREET.

1890.

CONTENTS.

Zionward.

A

" And I heard the voice of harpers harping with their harps ;
and they sung as it were a new song before the throne."

—Rev. xiv. 2, 3.

"Until the day break, and the shadows flee away."

—CANT. ii. 17.

I.

HARK ! hark ! 'tis music sweet,
   And harps are loudly ringing ;
Whence come the joyful strains,
   My weary hours are bringing ?
O ! are those harps the golden harps ?
   And are the angels singing ?

II.

List ! from the hills they come—
   Nay, higher yet, and higher ;
Ah ! 'tis no earthly strain,
   That fills me with desire ;
'Tis angel voices on the wind,
   And ah ! they're coming nigher.

3

III.

O angels bright and fair!
  Fain would I join your singing,
But I must tarry all the night,
  E'en while your harps are ringing;
But the night is dying, and the morn
  A brighter day is bringing.

IV.

Wakes now the Eternal day!
  From earth, oh bear me higher!
Beyond the gold-tipped hills,
  Up to the heavenly choir;
I hear their voices on the wind,
  And ah! they're coming nigher.

Morning.

" I cannot ope mine eyes
But thou art ready there to catch
My morning soul and sacrifice :
That we must needs for that day make a match.

  * * * * * *

Teach me Thy love to know ;
That this new light which now I see,
May both the work and workman show ;
Then by a sunbeam I will climb to Thee."

        —HERBERT.

I.

BRIGHTLY from the gold-tipped hills,
   Morning comes with matins singing ;
Every heart with gladness fills,
   And the leafy bowers are ringing ;
Nature opes her slumbering eye,
   Morn is smiling in the sky.

II.

Let us join the cheerful song,
   Nature sings in early morning ;
May its echoes all day long,
   Every deed of life adorning,
Cheer us on our pilgrim way,
   Till the evening bids us stay.

III.

Fill our hearts with morning light,
   Lord, who givest light and gladness;
May the sorrows of the night
   Never more afflict with sadness;—
So when darkness falls around,
   Light shall in our hearts be found.

VI.

Soon shall break the fairest morn
   Ever shone from hill tops golden,
And Eternal day adorn
   Zion, with her bulwarks olden;—
Pilgrim, lo, the brightening skies!
   Soon the Eternal day shall rise.

Evening.

"Sun of my soul ! Thou Saviour dear,
  It is not night if Thou be near ;
  O, may no earth-born cloud arise
  To hide Thee from Thy servant's eyes."

—KEBLE.

" In the shadow of Thy wings will I rejoice."

—Ps. lxiii. 7.

I.

COME rest awhile, 'tis eventide—
    The hour to meditation dear;
And set the cares of life aside,
      For God is near.

II.

O let a thankful spirit tell
    The wonders of His heavenly grace;
The love that loves us, all too well,
      Who spurn His grace.

III.

Amid our daily life He bears
    Our cold despite and thankless scorn;
As if He gave not rest at eve,
      And joy at morn.

IV.

Thou gav'st me, Lord, at early morn,
   A gift unsullied, for my care,—
Another day, I might adorn
     With graces rare.

V.

I dare not tell it to my God,
   But O that gift's no longer bright;
He gave it with the charm of morn,
     And now 'tis night.

VI.

O God, 'tis well at eventide,
   The hour for meditation given,
To know we're welcome at Thy side,—
     Foretaste of Heaven.

VII.

For O, one precious day misspent,
   Is all too great a load to bear;
But I will lay it at Thy feet,
     And leave it there.

"At evening time it shall be light."
—Zech. xiv. 7.

I.

Another day is ended,
  My God, I'll sing to Thee ;
Thou hast my way attended,
  When dangers frowned on me ;
Now may Thy love Thy servant keep,
Refresh, and bless, with kindly sleep.

II.

Another day is ended ;
  My sin I here deplore—
What's done may not be mended,
  But I would sin no more.
Now let Thy grace my sin forgive,
And teach Thy servant how to live.

13

III.

O Thou who never sleepest,
  To whom the night is day !
O Thou who Israel keepest
  By Thy strong hand alway !
Now let Thy light around me shine,
And guard with that strong hand of Thine.

IV.

When life's short day is ended,
  And death's dark night is near ;
From Satan's power defended,
  O may I banish fear,—
And with the morn's Eternal light,
Begin the day that has no night.

Flight of Time.

"So teach us to number our days, that we may apply our hearts unto wisdom."—Ps. xc. 12.

Καὶ τοῦτο, εἰδότες τὸν καιρὸν, ὅτι ὥρα ἡμᾶς ἤδη ἐξ ὕπνου ἐγερθῆναι· νῦν γὰρ ἐγγύτερον ἡμῶν ἡ σωτηρία, ἢ ὅτε ἐπιστεύσαμεν.

—ROMANS xiii. 11.

"Thou shalt guide me with Thy counsel, and afterwards receive me to glory."—Ps. lxxiii. 24.

I.

THE seasons come and go,
　　The years are born and die ;
And quickly flies our little life,
Its love, its hate, its peace, its strife,
　　And in the grave we lie.

II.

The seasons come and go,—
　　Another year is gone ;
I could unlive it every day,
But Christ hath shown a better way,
　　That brings me to the throne.

III.

O give me wisdom, Lord,
　　My little life to spend,
As those who seek eternal bliss,
Nor linger in a world like this,
　　Whose blessing has an end.

IV.

There is eternal day ;
　　There is eternal love ;
And nothing that can wound or grieve,
Or cloud with sorrow or deceive,
　　Can enter heaven above.

V.

O life, thou art not long !
　　O death, thou'rt ever near !
But I will wait, and work, and sing,
Till death the welcome warrant bring,
　　Which Christ has stripped of fear.

VI.

Till then, my Lord, be near,
　　And with Thy counsel guide :
O bring me daily nearer God,—
Though dark the sky, and rough the road,—
　　Where I shall aye abide.

Communion.

" Here Thy chosen and worthy servants partake of that heavenly food which nourishes their souls to life immortal, while reprobate and bold intruders take empty elements void of spiritual substance and saving power. This is a mystery above our comprehension. This kindles in us holy zeal, and engages our devoutest affections. And by receiving creatures, in themselves of mean and common efficacy, we find our weaknesses strengthened, our decays recruited, and our love of Thee and virtue strangely heightened and confirmed."—À KEMPIS.

"My flesh is meat indeed, and My blood is drink indeed."
—JOHN vi. 55.

"This do in remembrance of Me."—LUKE xxii. 19.

I.

WE bless Thee, Lord, that Thou hast spread
　A table for Thy people here ;
Where we may taste the living bread,
　And feel Thy blessed presence near.

II.

Here, where Thy people meet, Thou art,
　We hear Thy voice in accents sweet ;
Thy blood is wine to fainting heart,
　Thy flesh to hungry spirits meat.

III.

O help us, Lord, to feast with joy
　Upon the bounties of Thy grace :
Here may no anxious thoughts annoy,
　Here may we see Thy loving face.

IV.

O Christ, who, in Thy love untold,
  Didst give Thyself to death for man,
Here at Thy table, Lord, unfold
  The beauty of Redemption's plan.

V.

O send Thy Spirit to our aid,—
  That Spirit promised long ago,
When first the solemn feast was laid,
  Even in the valley of Thy woe.

VI.

And let Him bring sweet comfort near,
  That when we see the thorn-decked brow,
We may remember He who died
  Is crowned with life immortal now.

Submission.

"O what owe I to the file, to the hammer, to the furnace of my Lord Jesus! Grace tried is better than grace, and it is more than grace: it is glory in its infancy."

—SAMUEL RUTHERFORD.

I.

WE praise Thee, Lord, for every joy of life ;
  For every song the smiling summer sings ;
For every hour of peace in midst of strife,
  And all the sweetness of earth's pleasant things.

II.

We praise Thee, Lord, that on our upward way
  The clouds o'ertake us, and the night is sad ;
That fears afflict us with a sore dismay,
  And rob the bosom of the peace we had.

III.

Yea, Lord, we thank Thee, if our hopes decay,
  And, all unmindful of our earnest prayer,
Thou sendest bitter things for sweet, each day,
  For gladness sorrow, and for comfort care.

25

IV.

For Thou art Wisdom, and Thou doest best;
  Thou dost not wound us that the heart may pine;
Thou sendest trouble that the soul may rest,
  Where trouble comes not, in Thy love divine.

V.

Send what Thou wilt, Thy wisdom make the
    choice;—
  Thy rod to wound us, if our life rebel;
Thy joy to cheer us—we shall aye rejoice,
  For what Thou doest, Lord, Thou doest well.

"The joy of the Lord is your strength."—NEH. viii. 10.

"Ye shall weep and lament, but the world shall rejoice; and ye shall be sorrowful, but your sorrow shall be turned into joy."
—JOHN xvi. 20.

I.

'TIS not the sparkling joy of life,
That girds the soul with lasting strength,
To live the Christ-like life on earth,
And win the rest of God at length.

II.

The smiles of those our spirits love
May cheer us as a summer day:
But e'en when summer smiles on earth,
The heart may mourn the hours away.

III.

Wouldst thou be glad? then learn to weep:
Joy comes from grief, and smiles from tears:
There's richer joy in one sad hour,
Than in the mirth of countless years.

IV.

Live not for self: 'tis hard to crush
    The bounding heart that upward flies ;
But ere the Christ within us lives,
    The life of self within us dies.

V.

Wouldst thou be glad ? then learn to weep :
    Self is not slain with tearless eyes ;
But from the loss of earth and time,
    The lasting joys of heaven arise.

VI.

Cheered by that hope the heart is strong—
    Yea, e'en in weakness we have strength,—
To live the Christ-like life on earth,
    And win the rest of God at length.

Adoration.

" I will bless the Lord at all times ; His praise shall continually be in my mouth. My soul shall make her boast in the Lord : the humble shall hear thereof and be glad. O magnify the Lord with me, and let us exalt His name together."—Ps. xxxiv. 1-3.

> "Let them praise the name of the Lord : for His name alone is excellent ; His glory is above the earth and heaven."
>
> —Ps. cxlviii. 13.

I.

WORSHIP God, O earth adore Him,
Hills, and vales, and woods, and streams ;
Come and lay your gifts before Him,
Pleasant lands where pleasure dreams ;
'Tis His grace that decks your brow,
Lay your gifts before Him now.

II.

Worship God, O summer gladness,
Decked with blossoms all aglow ;
Worship God, O winter sadness,
Hail, and wind, and frost, and snow ;
Worship God with praises meet,
Pay your homage at His feet.

III.

Worship God, O sea adore Him,
With your waters calm and bright ;
Spread your ripples out before Him,
Let them sparkle in His sight ;

31

Let your billows tempest driven,
Shout His praise who rules in Heaven.

IV.

Sons of men, to whom from glory
   Christ the Son of God came down ;
Tell in songs the wondrous story
   Of the cross, the grave, the crown ;
Sing the praise of Him who died,
Jesus Christ the Crucified.

V.

Worship God, ye saints adore Him,
   Tune your harps to highest strains ;
Humbly cast your crowns before Him,
   Who hath burst the tyrants' chains ;
Praise our God who victory won,
Praise the Father, praise the Son.

VI.

God, Creator, wise and glorious,
   All creation homage pays :
God, Redeemer, strong, victorious,
   Saints surround Thee with their praise ;
Heaven and earth, united, bring
Homage to their God and King.

"The Heavens declare the glory of God."—Ps. xix. I.

" All Thy works shall praise Thee, O Lord."—Ps. cxlv. 10.

I.

O GOD, Thy glory gilds the sun,
    And gives the stars their light ;
They bring us joy to cheer the day,
    And peace to calm the night,—
Where'er their rays in silence fall,
We see Thy glory in them all.

II.

O God, Thy beauty paints the earth,
    And gives the flowers their glow,
On harvest fields Thy wealth abounds ;
    And when our barns o'erflow,
The riches of the God of Heaven
Are freely to His servants given.

III.

Thy voice is in the thunder roll,
    That rends the forest trees;
We hear it as a voice of love,
    In every whispering breeze;
In every song the warbler trills,
In harmony of mountain rills.

IV.

O God, we see Thee everywhere,
    Thy glory gives us light;
Thy beauty paints the summer fields
    With flowers and pastures bright.
In every sound that bids rejoice,
We hear the great Creator's voice.

The Love of God.

" How excellent is Thy loving-kindness, O God! therefore the children of men put their trust under the shadow of Thy wings."

—Ps. xxxvi. 7.

I.

LOVE is no attribute of Thine,
  But Thou art love, the source and sum,
And from that plenitude divine,
  My kindest thoughts and wishes come,
As from the sun's bright orb is given
  The light that fills the earth and heaven.

II.

My God, how comforting the thought,
  How full of strength for every day,
That Thou art love, and changest not,
  A strong support, a lasting stay;
Eternal God, I rest in Thee,
  Whose love is from Eternity.

III.

My God is love; hence would I see,
  My sin no trifle, passing small,
But deep ingratitude to Thee,
  Who lov'st the sinner through it all;

37

And by that love persistent, broad,
　　Would'st win the erring back to God.

IV.

Cease, heart, to fret !　If God be love,
　　My course through life is wisely led ;
The Eye that watches from above
　　In love directs the way I tread ;—
My plans may ripen to decay,
　　But God is love who maps my way.

V.

My God, the darkest night has stars,
　　If on Thy love I safe recline ;
No bitter, weeping sorrow, mars
　　The image of the life divine ;
Thy love, O God, the sorrow brings,
　　To win the heart from earthly things.

I.

O God, how kind thou art!
  Thy love, how passing great!
Not seraph tongue, nor human voice,
  Can half that love relate.

II.

'Tis higher than the stars,
  'Tis broader than the sea,
'Tis deeper than the deepest mine,
  This love of God for me.

III.

My heart was hard and cold,
  My mind was chained with doubt,
Till from Thy heart, as from an orb,
  The beams of love shone out.

39

IV.

The chains of doubt were loosed,
  My heart with love was fired,
And now I live that truer life,
  The love of God inspired.

V.

O God, how kind thou art!
  Thy love, how passing great!
To think upon my erring heart,
  And pity my estate;

VI.

To love, to stoop, to bless,—
  O love, how deep, how broad!
'Tis higher than the stars of night,
  This wondrous love of God.

VII.

Love, be my song alway,—
  Nay, can my lips be dumb?
I'll tell the wondrous love of God,
  Till to His rest I come.

I.

THY mercy, Lord, is like the sun,
  Whose light in distant ages shone,
And brightly gilds the years that run,
  From radiant skies ;
And only sinks when day is done,
  With morn to rise.

II.

O mercy lasting, changeless, sure !—
  A mercy only God could show,—
Through all those ages to endure,
  Of man's despite ;
Shall not that love my soul allure ?
  Ah ! well it might.

III.

Methought Thy mercy clean had gone,
  My hateful sin so hateful grew;
But morn arose, and forth it shone
  With glorious ray;
I felt myself in night, alone,
  And now 'tis day.

IV.

I'll praise Thy mercy every day,
  O God of mercy, lasting, sure!
That could for hate such love repay,
  Nor heed my lack,
That found me wounded, sad, astray,
  And brought me back.

I.

O LOVE that lingerest by my side
  And bear'st my burden every day,—
A light Thou art my steps to guide,
  And cheer my way.

II.

O love that, when the heart is sore,
  In lonely hours of deep regret,—
Tell'st of the heart that sorrow bore,
  And would not fret.

III.

O love that, when I blindly stray
  On many a false and devious track,
Still lingerest by me all the way,
  To win me back.

43

IV.

O love that when, by guilt oppressed,
   I fear the anger of my God,
Point'st to the Cross, where sore distressed
   Love bare the rod.

V.

O love that lingerest by my side,
   Find in my heart a resting-place ;
And in my life for aye abide,
   And shed Thy grace.

Carmina Christo.

Καὶ καλέσεις τὸ ὄνομα αὐτοῦ 'ΙΗΣΟΥΝ' αὐτὸς γὰρ σώσει τὸν λαὸν αὐτοῦ ἀπὸ τῶν ἁμαρτιῶν αὐτῶν.—MATT. i. 21.

"I dare say that angels' pens, angels' tongues, nay as many worlds of angels as there are drops of water in all the seas, and fountains, and rivers of the earth, cannot paint Him out to you."

—SAMUEL RUTHERFORD.

I.

I BROUGHT my darkest sin to mind,
    And called it by the vilest name,
And thought to fill my soul with grief
    When I had charged it with the blame;—
I said, "Before my God I'll fall,"
But sorrow came not at my call.

II.

I said, "Ah, soul! the wrath of God
    Shall smite the sinner with dismay;
The record of thy sin is kept,
    And swiftly nears the reckoning day;"—
Methought I heard God's thunders roll,
But sorrow came not to my soul.

III.

" Ah, stony heart ! can thought of sin
　　In all its vileness bring no tears ?
And canst thou hear God's thunders speak,
　　And weep not though the reckoning nears ? "
I had no weeping to control,
For sorrow came not to my soul.

IV.

I looked,—my Saviour looked on me ;—
　　O look of love, no heart can bear !
Like raging torrents came my tears,
　　And plunged my spirit in despair ;
Vain, vain my weeping to control,
For sorrow now has found my soul.

I.

O Christ, Thy love is wonderful,
  What mind its breadth can measure ?
A gem of rich and peerless worth,
  A rare and priceless treasure ;
There is no joy of earth so true,
  So full of lasting pleasure.

II.

The love of earth can ebb and flow,—
  It is not always flowing ;
The love of Christ, like morning sun,
  Is bright, and brighter growing
And from the noontide never fades,
  No sombre twilight knowing.

III.

The earth has gems of richest glow,
  And purest gold and rarest,—
O earthly pride! the worth may fade
  Of every gem thou wearest;
The love of Christ surpasses gold,
  And earthly gem the fairest.

IV.

The joys of earth, like summer flowers,
  May for a season please us;
But autumn comes, and winter's gloom,
  And grief and sorrow seize us;
Our joys lie withered in the tomb,
  Yet lives the love of Jesus.

V.

O Christ, Thy love is wonderful,
  What mind its breadth can measure?
Be it my gem of peerless worth,
  My rare and priceless treasure;
My joy, than joys of earth more rare,
  And full of lasting pleasure.

I.

REST to the weary heart,
  Soothing and calm ;
Love to the wounded heart,
  Healing and balm ;
Jesus, how sweet Thou art !
Rest to the weary heart.

II.

Peace to the troubled mind :
  Tempests are still ;
Light to the doubting mind,
  Teaching Thy will ;
Jesus, Thou art most kind !
Peace to the troubled mind.

III.

Joy to the pilgrim heart,
　　Song by the way ;
Guide to the seeking heart,
　　Fearful to stray ;
Jesus, how kind Thou art !
Joy to the pilgrim heart.

IV.

Dower of the needy soul,
　　Brother and Friend ;
Heaven of the trusting soul,
　　Life without end ;
Jesus, how kind Thou art !
Friend of the human heart

" Casting all your care upon Him ; for He careth for you."

—I PET. v. 7.

I.

HERE at the cross I lay my burden down,
  Here would I rest and feel my calm complete ;
Love lingers near, no chill rebuke, no frown ;
  Warm welcome greets me at the Saviour's feet.

II.

See on the cross the Man of Sorrows bears
  All sin's dark load, its burden and its shame ;
There are my sins, my sorrows, and my cares,
  Bound to His cross who took the sinner's name.

III.

Joy fills my soul : O Christ, whose love untold
  Bore to the cross my weary load of care !
Thee will I praise who didst that love unfold,
  When sad and lone at heart I found me there.

53

IV.

Here at the cross I would my life begin,
  Here would I take my cross and follow Thee ;
As Thou hast died, so will I die to sin,
  As Thou dost live, my life henceforth shall be.

"This is the day which the Lord hath made ; we will rejoice and be glad in it."—Ps. cxviii. 24.

I.

Oh let our hearts be joyful,
    Our joy in songs ascend,
For Christ arose victorious,
    And lives our lasting Friend ;
Nor death, nor grave, nor Satan,
    Could hold our Lord in chains,
He burst their bands asunder,
    And now immortal reigns.

II.

Who now shall fear the terror
    That haunts the silent tomb ?
For life hath stirred its silence,
    And lit its dismal gloom ;
The reign of death is ended,
    The reign of life begun,
For Christ to heaven ascended
    Hath life for mortals won.

III.

O day of days most gladsome!
  Thine hours encircle joy
That heaven can only perfect,
  And earth can ne'er annoy;
No shadow mars thy brightness,
  For nought can come between
The Christ that lives in glory,
  And earth, where Christ hath been.

"For we have not an High Priest who cannot be touched with a feeling of our infirmities."—HEB. iv. 15.

"I have laid help upon one that is mighty."—Ps. lxxxix. 19.

I.

THOU wilt not scorn me, Lord,
  If to Thy feet I bear
My every doubt and fear,
  My every grief and care—
Thou'lt give me comfort for my fear,
And bid my sorrow disappear.

II.

Thou knowest the burdened sigh,
  The throbbing heart, the woe,
For Thou art man, O Christ,
  And dweltst with man below;
Thou wert not free from human care,
Who not Thine own, but ours didst bear.

III.

Thou knowest the tempter's power,
   His subtil, luring art,
That wins, ah Lord! too soon,
   This foolish erring heart;
For Thou didst meet his cruel craft,
In pieces brake his poisoned shaft.

IV.

Thou knowest the night of doubt,
   That dreary, starless sky
That hides the face of God,
   And blinds the searching eye;
For Thou didst cry in sore dismay
When God had turned His face away.

V.

O Christ, I'll come to Thee,
   For Thou canst sympathise;
Thou art my brother man,
   Though now beyond the skies;
And Thou art strong the weak to aid,
And on Thy strength my help is laid.

"The Lord is my light and my salvation ; whom shall I fear ?"
—Ps. xxvii. 1.

I.

THE Lord is light about my path,
My Star, my Sun, to cheer me ;
The night is turned to day,
Its darkness flies away,
No terror can come near me.

II.

The Lord is light about my path,
Begone, then, doubt and sorrow !
I will not gaze through tears,
And mar my joys with fears
About the unknown morrow.

III.

The Lord is light about my path,
He's every day beside me—
From early morning ray,
Through all the hours of day,
And in the night He'll guide me.

IV.

The Lord is light about my path,—
His sun shall shine to-morrow,
And till my latest day
In twilight fades away,
And through earth's latest sorrow.

'Then He arose and rebuked the winds and the sea ; and there was a great calm."—MATT. ix. 26.

I.

O JESUS, let me hear Thy voice,—
    No music sweeter to my ear ;
It tells my drooping heart to hope,
    For Thou art near.

II.

Speak when the tempest fiercely blows,
    Bid Thou its angry raging cease,
For where Thy voice is heard, there reigns
    Eternal peace.

III.

Speak when the clouds in dusky folds
    Hide from mine eyes the noontide sun ;
For when Thy voice proclaims Thy will,
    Thy will is done.

IV.

O Jesus, let Thy voice be heard
In stilly eve and buoyant morn ;
And let the peace it brings, each day
My life adorn.

" When Christ, who is our life, shall appear, then shall ye also appear with Him in glory."—Col. iii. 4.

I.

WHEN the toil is ended
And the battle won,
Christ shall greet the victor
With the glad " Well done."
When the pilgrim journey
Every step is trod,
Then shall rest the pilgrim
In the home of God.

II.

When the will is moulded
To the will Divine,
And we crave no blessing,
Lord, that is not Thine ;
When Thy love reflected
In our life appears,
Heavenly hope disperses
Earthly doubts and fears.

III.

Till the toil is ended,
  Strengthen by Thine arm ;
Till the conflict's over,
  Keep us safe from harm ;
Till our pilgrim journey
  On the earth is past,
Tell us of the country
  Where we rest at last.

IV.

Bend, and mould, and fashion,
  Will and heart and mind ;—
Be Thy love, O Saviour,
  With our life entwined ;
Then when life is ended,
  And from earth we part,
We shall see and know Thee,
  Saviour, as Thou art.

"O send out Thy light and Thy truth."

—Ps. xliii. 3.

I.

Arise, O King of Zion !
And let Thy name be known ;
Take up the sceptre of Thy power,
And sit upon Thy throne.

II.

Claim Thou the heart's devotion,
The love of every soul ;
Bring strife and discord to an end,
And every will control.

III.

Where vice her hideous features
All unabashed reveals ;
Where pride and tyranny usurp,
And crush with iron heels ;

E

IV.

There let Thy voice be spoken,
  Give to the meek the crown ;
There let Thy mighty arm be raised,
  To cast the wicked down.

V.

Where men in darkness sitting
  Know not the glorious light ;
Where other kings usurp Thy place,
  There claim to rule by right.

VI.

Where frozen seas encircle
  A land of ageless snow ;
Where palm trees wave in sunny lands
  Where gems the rarest glow ;

VII.

On distant isles of ocean,
  Where fragrant breezes play,
And nature dreams the happy hours
  Of careless life away,

VIII.

There let Thy name be published
  Thou mighty Prince of Peace;
Begin the long predicted reign,
  That nevermore shall cease.

IX.

Arise, O King of Zion!
  And let Thy name be known;
Take up the sceptre of Thy power,
  And sit upon Thy throne.

"But He was wounded for our transgressions, He was bruised for our iniquities ; the chastisement of our peace was upon Him, and with His stripes we are healed."—ISA. liii. 5.

I.

On the Cross, the Saviour dying,
Wounded sore, and faint, and sighing,
Bowed beneath the burden lying
On His spotless soul.

II.

'Tis thy load He falters under ;
Speaks not Heaven in wrathful thunder ?
Earth ! behold the sight and wonder,
Love has borne the rod.

III.

Canst thou love the sin that bound Him,
Threw the robe of scorn around Him,
Mocking bowed the knee, and crowned Him
With the cruel thorn ?

IV.

Jesus, to Thy Cross relenting,
Bring I all my guilt repenting,
All my cruel sin lamenting,—
Christ, my sin forgive!

I.

JESUS, I will follow closely,
　Follow closely all the way,
Lest my erring foot should lead me
　From the heavenward path astray ;
Not to left or right I'd lean :
Plant my feet where Thine have been.

II.

Jesus, I will follow closely,
　For the night is coming down,
And the shadows cross the pathway,
　And the dark clouds grimly frown ;
If I lose Thee in the night,
Wouldst Thou find me in my plight ?

III.

Jesus, I will follow closely,
　Though the path be rough and long ;
If I faint Thou wilt not leave me,
　Kind Thy heart, Thy arm is strong ;

70

Sore the pathway, heart oppressed,
But my Leader leads to rest.

IV.

Jesus, I will follow closely,
 Singing gladly all the way ;
If I cease the song I'm singing,
 Seek me, I have gone astray ;
Pilgrim mercies make me strong,
Gird my loins, and tune my song.

V.

Jesus, I will follow closely,
 By-and-bye to enter in
Where the Pilgrim rests securely
 From his toil, and pain, and sin,—
'Mid the joys no heart can know,
Till it share the Pilgrim's woe.

PRINTED BY BALLANTYNE, HANSON AND CO.
EDINBURGH AND LONDON.